Cockatoo Magic

By Katharine Rogers
Illustrated By Nana Sakata

LOOSE
PARTS
PRESS

Loose Parts Press
PO Box 5
Lawson NSW 2783
ABN: 26 587 556 716
www.looseparts.com.au

Originally published by Loose Parts Press in 2022
Re-printed in 2024, hard cover edition

Book designed by Sharon Baldwin
Interior Fonts: Now, Open Sans Light, Moonlight
Cover Fonts: Railey, Moonlight

ISBN: 978-0-6455325-3-1
Printed by Rich Colour Printing

Published on unceded Darug and Gundungurra land. We pay our respects to the traditional custodians of the land and Aboriginal elders past, present and emerging.

To my grandmother Doris and my mum Jennifer,
who showed me what was possible.

-K.R.

To Nich, Ellie and Leo.

-N.S.

Little Ellie loves
to go exploring.

There's so much to see even in her own backyard.

Tiny ants. . .

Spotty ladybugs and. . .

SNOWY

the Sulphur-crested
cockatoo who comes
to visit every day.

Sometimes Snowy is cheeky and pulls washing off the line with his beak.

This makes Ellie laugh. . .
A LOT.

Ellie loves spending time with Snowy and she wishes they could go on big brilliant adventures together.

But Ellie doesn't feel brave enough for adventures outside her backyard.

Beyond the garden fence there are dogs, loud noises, and shadows.

"You can fly with me," says Snowy one day.

"No, people can't fly, except in planes or hot air balloons or helicopters," Ellie tells him.

"Grown-ups can't,
but kids can if we use
Cockatoo Magic,"
screeches Snowy.

Ellie gasps. "I've never heard of
Cockatoo Magic!"

"It's something only children can see," says Snowy.

With a whoosh, Snowy fans out the bright yellow feathers on top of his head. . .

and he SQUEAKS

and he SQUAWKS

and he SCREECHES

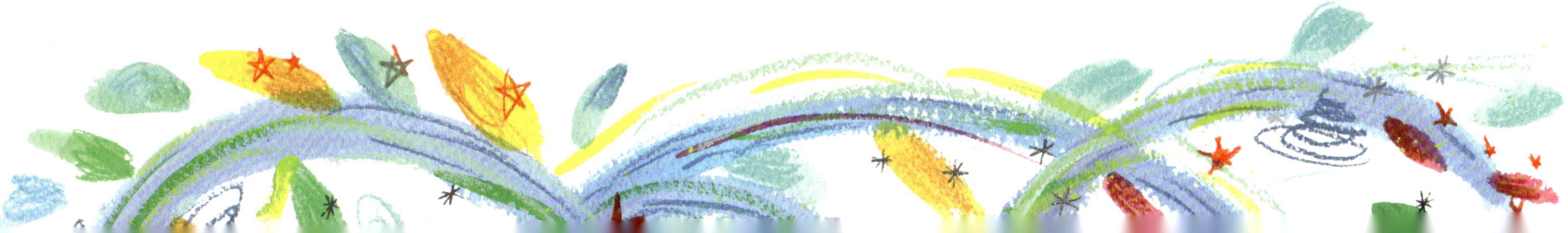

SQUEAK
SQUAWK
SCREECH

Suddenly Ellie shrinks down to the size of a rainbow lorikeet.

"Oh, I'm even smaller than you," Ellie giggles.

"That's cockatoo magic."

"Hop on, we'll go for a ride," squawks Snowy.

Ellie tries to climb on his back, but at first, it's not easy.

She slips, and she slides,
and she wiggles right off.

Finally, after lots of tries, she makes it and away they go!

They swoop over the
garden fence...

They sail past treetops. . .
They soar over the park.

"Let's play on the
swings," calls Ellie.

"Hold on tight, we're going down," screeches Snowy.
He spreads his wings wide and they glide to the ground.

Ellie slides down Snowy's back like a slippery dip,
landing with a plop in a soft pile of leaves.

Snowy flaps his yellow head feathers,

and he SQUEAKS
and he SQUAWKS
and he SCREECHES

Just
like that
Ellie returns
to her full size.

Ellie runs excitedly to play on the swings but somewhere nearby they can hear barking.

"We should see what all the noise is about," says Snowy.

"I don't like loud noises, I want to stay here," Ellie says.

Snowy flies in the direction of the barking and sees a puppy with her leg stuck in a bramble bush.

"I'm stuck and I've lost my humans. Can you help me?" barks the puppy.

Snowy launches into action. He flies back to Ellie to tell her the news.

"You must come quickly, Ellie," says Snowy.

"But the barking - it's too scary," says Ellie.

"I know things can
be scary sometimes,
but this dog won't
harm you. She needs
our help," says Snowy.

"I don't know. . .
I'm only little," says Ellie.

"Yes but you have a kind heart and a bright mind which makes you as big as the tallest tree," says Snowy.

"Okay," says Ellie. She takes a deep breath and runs to the puppy.

Snowy flies overhead squawking, "You can do it, Ellie. I know you can."

When Ellie reaches the puppy she carefully looks to see what the matter is, then takes a stick and slowly untangles the puppy's fur from the bramble.

"Oh, well done Ellie," cheers Snowy.

Ellie and Snowy guide the
puppy back to the path.
The puppy spots her humans
and runs to
greet them.

"Thank you," calls the puppy
as she disappears into the distance.

The sun is beginning to set. Feeling much braver, Ellie wishes they could go on more adventures right now.

But she can feel her tummy rumbling and thinks it must be time for dinner, so...

with a SQUEAK
and a SQUAWK
and a SCREECH

. . . the two friends head for home, with
the sound of cockatoo magic lingering in the air.

What amazing adventures will they go on tomorrow?